CARTER

—— and the ——

CURIOUS MAZE

Other Weird Stories Gone Wrong:

Jake and the Giant Hand
Myles and the Monster Outside

CARTER

—— and the ——

CURIOUS MAZE

PHILIPPA
DOWDING

Illustrations by Shawna Daigle

DUNDURN
TORONTO

Project Editor: Carrie Gleason
Editor: Allister Thompson
Illustrator: Shawna Daigle
Interior Design: Laura Boyle
Cover Design: Courtney Horner
Cover art by Shawna Daigle
Printer: Webcom

Library and Archives Canada Cataloguing in Publication
Dowding, Philippa, author
        Carter and the curious maze / Philippa Dowding.

(Weird stories gone wrong)

Issued in print and electronic formats.
ISBN 978-1-4597-3249-0 (paperback).--ISBN 978-1-4597-3250-6 (pdf).--
ISBN 978-1-4597-3251-3 (epub)

        I. Title. II. Series: Dowding, Philippa, 1963- . Weird stories gone wrong.

PS8607.O9874C37 2016   jC813'.6   C2015-906602-6
                                            C2015-906603-4

1 2 3 4 5   20 19 18 17 16

We acknowledge the support of the **Canada Council for the Arts** and the **Ontario Arts Council** for our publishing program. We also acknowledge the financial support of the **Government of Canada** through the **Canada Book Fund** and **Livres Canada Books**, and the **Government of Ontario** through the **Ontario Book Publishing Tax Credit** and the **Ontario Media Development Corporation**.

The author would like to thank the Writers' Reserve Program of the Ontario Arts Council for their support.

VISIT US AT
Dundurn.com | @dundurnpress | Facebook.com/dundurnpress | Pinterest.com/dundurnpress

Dundurn
3 Church Street, Suite 500
Toronto, Ontario, Canada
M5E 1M2

For C and S,
always amazing

THIS PART IS (MOSTLY) TRUE

You should know, before you even start this book, that it's a little scary. And parts of it are even a bit weird and strange. I wish I could make the story less scary and strange, but this is the way I heard it, so I really have no choice.

It starts like this:

A long time ago, a little old man planted a garden maze. It was a special walking path through bushes, and it was very peaceful. The man invited his neighbours to come and walk through the maze any time of day or night. The neighbours enjoyed it.

For a while.

The maze grew and grew at an astonishing, even unnatural pace. It was whispered that the old man had a magical connection to the soil. Some thought he had an enchanted water supply or perhaps bewitched garden implements. It was true that he carried a pair of red-handled garden shears with him wherever he went, and he guarded them closely. Whatever the case, the man could make anything grow.

He had what people call a "green thumb."

Which was unfortunate, since it also happened that his REAL thumb was terribly deformed and crooked. It was huge and stuck out at a strange angle from his hand. The man hid his horrible thumb. Some people said his thumb was a curse, others said it was just an unfortunate birth defect, and not to be cruel.

And *some* people said if you looked too closely you could see … leaves growing out of it.

Whatever people said, the truth was that everything the man planted turned green, leafy, and lush. But soon the maze became too green and leafy and lush. It was overgrown and wild, and people started to see and hear strange … things … in there.

The bushes in the maze grew and grew.

Here's the weird and scary part. One sunny summer day, a child wandered into the maze ... and was never the same. When she came back out, she told a mysterious story about strange lands and travelling through time. Which no one believed, of course, since she was only in the maze for about ten minutes. But then more children went into the maze, and when they came back out ... a few of *them* told strange stories, too. After a while, the authorities came to have a serious talk to the old man with the green thumb, and ... there was no sign of him. Or his maze. The old man and the maze had simply vanished, and no one heard or saw him ever again.

You don't have to believe this story. But just because things are odd or a little strange or unbelievable doesn't always make them untrue. Truth is an odd thing; one person's truth can be another person's lie. That's the most important thing to remember about this story: sometimes things that seem like lies are actually true. And sometimes you never can tell.

That's the spookiest thing of all.

CHAPTER 1

SO NOT SCARY

The mummy howled.

Carter yawned.

The skeleton rattled.

Carter sneezed.

The ghost flapped in his face.

Carter rolled his eyes.

He had to face it: the haunted house at the fair just wasn't scary anymore.

It used to be scary when he was a little kid. Even last year, when he was eleven, it was still a little creepy. But this year?

No chills, no goosebumps, no shrieks, nothing. The only thing Carter noticed was that the pop-up crypt keeper had a broken spring sticking out of his head, and the floating ghost was covered in a thick layer of dust. Plus, there was a bored-looking man standing behind the curtain near the end of the ride, beside a red button that said, "In Case of Emergency, Push to STOP."

What emergency? Carter thought. *Not even a little kid would be scared by this boring ride!*

The haunted house ride ended, and Carter climbed out of the rolling car. He pushed past the bored fair worker and shoved his way through the crowd into the bright sunshine. It was weird out in the noisy midway after the dark of the haunted house.

Carter scanned the crowd and found his older sister, Sydney, but frankly, she would have been hard to miss. She was wearing a ridiculous red hat with googly eyes and long, red tentacles.

"What the heck is *that* thing?" Carter asked as he joined her. It was the weirdest hat he'd ever seen.

"It's a squid hat," Sydney answered, pleased. "I won it. Over there." She pointed at a tent with stripes on it under an old tree. "While you were in the haunted house," she added.

"Take it off, you look strange," Carter said. Everything about the fair suddenly seemed strange. His once-favourite haunted house. And now the weirdest hat in the world.

And there were more things that suddenly didn't seem so fun. For one thing, it was too hot. And for another, it was too loud. He'd never noticed how loud and hot the fair was before. Plus the place smelled. The air was full of the reek of fried food and garbage.

Yep ... that's garbage, all right.

Carter and Sydney walked out of the noisy, hot midway and bought ice cream cones. They sat on a picnic bench near the lake beside an enormous grey rock.

The water lay perfectly still against the pebbles on the shore. It looked pretty, but the water smelled like goose poop, which Carter had never noticed before. A few sailboats bobbed in the lake, but there was no wind. It was too hot and still, even for the sailboats.

Carter looked up at the huge grey rock beside them. It stood above his head, above his arms, stretched out. It looked very old and was covered with moss and deep scratches near the top. He finished his ice cream and studied the huge rock.

I'm so bored, I'm studying rocks! I have to get out of here!

"Come on, Sydney, let's go find Mom," he begged. "I'm dying of boredom! This place is dull. Nothing interesting has ever happened here in the history of the world. Let's go!"

"It's not boring, and Mom's not meeting us at the parking lot for a little while, Carter. What's wrong with you? There's still so much to see." Sydney marched away. Carter sighed and followed her past the tents and midway rides.

Then he stopped.

Someone was watching him. Across the grass beside a tall tree, a stranger waved and beckoned. Carter was too far away to tell if the man — because it looked like a very small man in a long green smock — was waving at him or someone else. Carter slowly raised his hand and cautiously waved back.

The man waved again, more urgently this time.

Carter looked around to see if the person was waving at someone behind him, but no, he was alone. How odd. Who could that be? He didn't know anyone else at the fair. Carter realized that Sydney was getting farther away; her red hat bounced in the distance.

He ran to catch up with his sister, looking over his shoulder once more ... but the stranger in the green smock was gone.

CHAPTER 2

DULL, DULL, DULL

Carter walked to catch up with Sydney as quickly as he could.

How weird! Who was that man, and why was he waving at me?

Other people had fun at the fair, just not him. The Double Helix Death-Defying roller coaster rattled overhead, filled with shrieking people. The Skull-N-Bonz Pirate Ship swung from side-to-side, filled with more loud fairgoers. Riders screamed on the Monster Loop-the-Loop or from inside the Zippedy Spinner boxes as they spun in circles. Everyone was having fun. Everyone but him.

Instead, he got stuck with dull, not-haunted rides and weird, waving strangers. He caught up to Sydney, who was reading a signpost.

"Look, Carter! *The Curious Maze: The Most Interesting Ride You'll Ever Take.* I've never seen this here before," Sydney said, pointing at the sign.

"What's a ... curious maze?" Carter asked. *Not that I care!*

"It's a hedge of bushes, on a winding path," she answered.

Carter moaned. "I know what a maze is, but why is it curious?"

Sydney ignored him and read the rest of the sign out loud:

"*Welcome to the Curious Maze.*
Walk the path,
Clear your mind,
Reach the end,
See what you find!"

"Well, that still doesn't tell us anything. What's curious about it?" Carter complained.

"Why don't you walk the maze and see?" a voice said, making Carter jump. The voice came from the other side of the bushes.

"Hello?" Carter called. There was no answer.

Sydney took a few steps into the maze with Carter close behind her. The bushes followed a brick pathway that wound back and forth and then disappeared around a corner. The maze was green and leafy and looked just a tiny bit inviting.

"Hello?" Carter called again, a little louder.

A voice answered ahead of them this time, an old man's voice, just of out sight around a bend in the path. "You'll have to come in further. I'm over here," the old voice croaked.

Sydney and Carter took a few more steps. It was quiet and surprisingly cool inside the maze. Suddenly, the heat of the day fell away.

"What's ... what's a curious maze?" Carter called out.

A man appeared right behind them, an old, old man, holding a huge pair of red-handled garden shears. Carter whirled around and gasped. *Where'd he come from? Out of the hedge?*

The old man was tiny and bent. He wore a long green smock almost to his knees and clutched the garden shears by his side. Carter had never seen such an old man. He looked like he was made out of wood, he was so gnarled and bent and warped, just like an old tree. There was something terribly wrong with one of his thumbs. It was far too large, and Carter wasn't sure but it looked almost ... green ... and *leafy*.

Carter looked away, trying not to stare.

"Hello," the old man rustled. "I'm the maze-keeper. You can call me Mr. Green."

"Oh ... hello. That was you just now, beside the tree, waving at me?" Mr. Green blinked and looked at Carter and then nodded ever so slightly.

"Can I help you? Did you want something?" Carter asked.

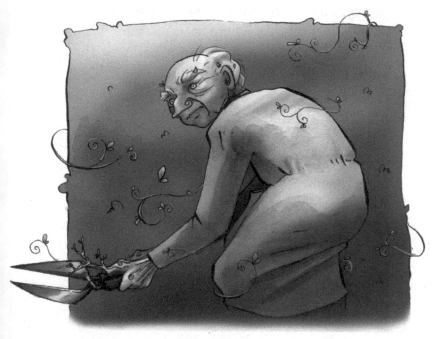

"I wanted you to discover the curious maze." The old man clutched his garden shears, and Carter tried not to look at his weird thumb.

"Well, what's a curious maze anyway? Your sign doesn't say, doesn't really explain it," Carter answered, struggling to remain polite while he rolled his eyes away from the strange hand.

The old man grinned, and Carter thought the ancient face was going to crack like tree bark.

"A maze is a pathway. Some people think it represents a meditation, or a journey. If something is troubling you, you walk along the path and see where it takes you. What could be more curious than a pathway that calms your troubles?" the old man said.

Mr. Green.

Now the old man was closer, there was definitely something off about him, and it wasn't just his thumb. He was ... creaking, almost like you could blow him over with a strong breeze. And then there was the small fact of the creepy thumb sticking out of the sleeve of his smock, grasping at the garden shears. Funny, thought Carter, that when you try NOT to stare at a thing, sometimes it's all you can see.

Mr. Green caught Carter staring and pulled his thumb up his sleeve.

"Why don't you just walk the maze? It's very *interesting*," the old man creaked.

"Um ..." Carter hesitated. "I should ask my sister. We really ... we really should be going to find our mom." He looked around for Sydney, but she was already disappearing down the pathway. Her tall red squid hat bobbed just above the bushes.

"Come on, Carter!" she called in a voice that sounded too far away. He didn't WANT to follow her into some boring garden maze.

He REALLY just wanted to go home ...

... when the old man cackled, and his laugh, if it WAS a laugh, sounded like a tree about to snap in the wind.

"It's the most *interesting* attraction at the fair, nothing dull about it," Mr. Green said. "I *promise!*"

Then Carter heard his sister call again, but this time she sounded REALLY far away.

Carter took three more steps into the pathway.

It's too quiet in here, and where's Sydney?

"Sydney!" he called. He couldn't see her squid hat over the top of the hedge anymore.

There was no answer.

Carter whirled around, but now the old man was gone, too. The bushes rose above his head, the brick pathway lay at his feet. He had no choice but to follow his sister. He took a few more steps and then started to walk.

Carter had entered the curious maze.

CHAPTER 3

CREEPY LEAF GIRL

Carter walked along the brick path-way between the tall hedges. Someone shrieked on a ride on the midway, but the sound was very far away.

"SYD-NEY!" he called, again and again, but no one called back. It got quieter and quieter. Soon all he could hear was the summer breeze rustling the leafy green bushes all around him.

He kept walking ...

... when a bush rustled beside him.

"Sydney?" he called.

No answer.

He called again, "Sydney? SYDNEY!"

Then very faintly he heard, "Carter! Over here!" He spun around and saw a tiny fleck of red over the top of the bushes.

Sydney's squid hat!

"SYDNEY! WAIT!" Carter ran toward the hat. But when he got there, he found nothing but bushes, more bushes, and the brick pathway on the ground.

Carter looked up at the sky. He'd stopped hearing the midway several minutes ago, but now he couldn't *see* the huge roller coasters, either. Which was weird. The only thing above him was blue sky and a few fluffy clouds.

Where did the monster roller coasters on the midway go? Where was the swinging pirate ship? And where was his sister?

He listened hard. Absolute silence. He strained his ears, but all he heard was the wind.

Then … footsteps.

"Sydney?" he called. Something about the place, about being all alone, was making him very jumpy.

A girl walked out of the bushes. She stopped and stared. Carter stared back.

Not Sydney.

The girl was about his age and wore a long, old-fashioned dress with a bonnet.

She must be a historical performer from the midway, Carter thought.

"H — hello? Have you seen my sister?" he said, trying to be polite. The girl stared. It took a moment for Carter to realize that there was something a bit ... strange ... about her. She had leaves in her bonnet, in her hair, and across the top of her shoulders.

And in her hands.

And *sprouting* out of her ears.

"What ... what do you want?" he asked, edging away.

Her bonnet fell back off her head. Her eyebrows! There was definitely something very wrong with her eyebrows. They ... they were green.

And GROWING!

The girl raised her arms toward Carter and dropped her head to one side. She walked forward and opened her mouth in a silent scream. A green leaf burst out of her tongue, over her lips, through her teeth ...

... Carter turned and ran.

She had a leaf SPROUTING OUT OF HER MOUTH!

He ran down the pathway as fast as he could, and he didn't look over his shoulder.

He'd never seen anything so weird in his life. *Who has leaves in their mouth?*

What the heck was wrong with her?

He ran through the maze, turning right and left blindly until he couldn't catch his breath, then he leaned over, gasping into his knees. When he straightened up, he called out, "Sydney? SYDNEY!" a few times, but there was no answer. Everything was very, very silent.

That girl, this place, it's too weird!

When he caught his breath, he noticed a pair of red-handled garden shears leaning up against the maze wall.

"Mr. Green? There's a very creepy, leafy girl in here, in old-fashioned clothes. And … and I can't find my sister! My mother will be looking for me soon. If you can hear me, I'd like to go home now! And I found your garden shears!" Carter was just about to pick them up when a weird, leafy thumb reached out of the hedge and snatched the shears away. Then the rest of the old man appeared and he tucked the garden shears into his smock pocket.

"No need to shout," the old man said.

Carter tried not to scream.

I'm not scared! No one can just materialize out of thin air, right?

"Okay, very funny, Mr. Green. Good one with the leafy historical performer girl back there. And I don't know how you got rid of all the midway noises or the huge roller coasters, or why it's so cool in here. Maybe we're hidden inside some big, secret air-conditioned building or something. But really, I just want to find my sister. I'm done with your curious maze. Which way is out?"

"So you saw the lost girl, did you?" The old man stared at Carter and opened and closed the red-handled garden shears, just once.

SNIP.

"Hmmm, how curious. Most people don't get to see *her*. She must have taken a special liking to you." Mr. Green raised his eyebrows at Carter. Awfully bushy, leafy eyebrows.

Carter frowned and backed away. He gulped.

Lost girl?

"Oh, right. Sure, ha-ha, she's some weird lost hedge girl, and only *special* people get to see her, I get it. Very funny, Mr. Green."

"Believe me, Carter, there's nothing funny about the curious maze."

"How … how do you know my name?"

"Oh, the maze told me."

Carter started to get just the tiniest prickle at this neck, like he should maybe be the faintest bit afraid. This old guy was creepy. Still, it wouldn't be hard for Mr. Green to figure out his name; he would have heard Sydney shouting it. The old man was doing a pretty convincing job of being weird and scary, though, Carter had to admit.

Carter darted his eyes at Mr. Green's thumb ... and quickly looked away. He kept his voice steady.

"Look, I really just want to get out of here. My mom's coming to get me soon. What's the trick?"

"Oh, there's no trick to it, Carter. It's really quite simple: just keep walking. Every maze is a journey. You just have to choose the right path. Hopefully, in your case, the choices you make won't be *too dull*." The old man turned his back on Carter and started to shuffle away.

"But how far is it?"

Mr. Green stopped and looked back. "Oh, that's up to you. Everyone finds a different pathway out of the maze. No doubt you'll bump into a few others looking for an end to it. Try not to be *too* bored now." Mr. Green rustled away.

Others?

Carter didn't like the sound of that at all. If there were "others" in the maze anything like the Creepy Leaf Girl, he'd just as soon not find out.

"Maybe I should just follow you back to the start?" Carter yelled after Mr. Green, who was disappearing around a leafy corner.

"You can try to follow me if you wish, but the rules are quite clear: you must go in only one direction, forward. Once you've entered the curious maze, it's a one-way journey to the end, I'm afraid. Your journey. You might not like the consequences if you try to go backward. And the maze definitely won't like it. But it's up to you." The old man's voice faded away.

"Rules? What rules? No one said anything about rules!" Carter yelled, alone once again. What did the old man mean, *You might not like the consequences?* Or the *maze* wouldn't like it?

That was crazy. It was slowly dawning on Carter that maybe Mr. Green was just crazy? All the more reason to get out of there as quickly as possible.

Carter made a decision: he'd follow Mr. Green. He took two steps backward …

… and yelped! The bushes rustled and rose up all around him in a tight, green wall. Vines curled out of the hedge and shook in his face, like fists shaking in anger.

Someone must be moving the hedge around!

There was NO way out now; the bushes held him tight. He called out, "Okay, Mr. Green. I get it! I won't try to trick the maze. It doesn't like it when I go backward. Like you said."

No one answered him.

The bushes moved away from Carter, and the pathway reappeared at his feet.

Time to be sneaky.

Carter pretended to take two steps forward, and then he spun around to follow Mr. Green one more time. But the bushes rose up faster this time, angry leaf fists shaking in his face … then everything went black.

CHAPTER 4

BOYS AND SOLDIERS

Carter opened his eyes. His head hurt, and he lay face down on the pathway. Vines from the hedge curled slowly around his feet and up his leg. As soon as he sat up, the vines quickly vanished back into the hedge.

Weird!

He sat up and groaned. He felt the back of his head: it had a bump on it.

Something hit me!

He opened and closed his eyes, trying to clear his blurry vision. The maze was a solid green wall all around him. There was no way out.

Then, suddenly, there was. He watched as a few bushes slid sideways, and a pathway appeared.

"Okay, so your employees are in leafy green suits back there, moving the bushes around. Good one again, Mr. Green," he said. But no one answered. All he heard was the wind. Then …

… SNIP!

He groaned and stood up, rubbing the back of his head. A brick from the pathway was out of place at his feet. Carter picked it up and heaved it a little, feeling the weight of it. The brick was definitely heavy enough to knock him out.

But it was also possible that when the hedge had reared up and scared him, he tripped over the brick and knocked *himself* out.

Who would bash me on the head? That's crazy. I must have tripped … right?

"You should probably tell your employees not to trip kids, Mr. Green," Carter called out. There was no answer.

He thought he heard a faint SNIP! on the other side of the hedge, but when he stood still and listened … there was nothing but silence. The pathway was ahead of him now, and there was only one direction to go.

This maze has to end sometime ... just keep walking. And try not to trip and knock yourself out or bump into Creepy Leaf Girl again.

Carter started walking. He was beginning to realize that a path in any direction was better than no path at all.

Then ... he heard it: "Carter! Carter!"

SYDNEY!

"HERE! I'M HERE! HELP! SYDNEY!" Carter ran down the pathway. He had to find his sister! He had to get out of there! He must be getting near the end of the stupid maze; he'd been running so long. He ran, calling for Sydney again and again ... but once again, there was no answer. She had vanished.

He wanted to scream in frustration. Instead, he stopped to catch his breath ... and the hedge right beside him rustled.

"Sydney?" he whispered. *Please be Sydney!*

Not Sydney.

A small boy popped his head through the hedge. He stared at Carter and then slowly stepped out onto the path. He was about five years old and wore short pants, a white shirt, and a matching jacket. He had a soft cap on his head and leather lace-up shoes. He wasn't covered in leaves, though, Carter quickly noted.

The little boy was wearing old-fashioned clothes, just like Creepy Leaf Girl. Maybe they were historical performers who had wandered away from some midway stage show?

Pretty *convincing* historical performers.

"Mummy?" the little boy sniffled. He rubbed his nose with a grubby hand and looked around.

Carter shook his head. "No. I'm Carter. Are you lost? Are you looking for your mom?"

The boy looked at Carter and nodded. He looked around once more and disappeared into the opposite hedge. Carter heard him say, "Mummy?" again, his voice more distant. Then the little boy was gone.

"Um, Mr. Green?" Carter shouted. "There's a lost kid in here! You should probably help him!" He considered following the little boy, maybe try to help him, but he didn't want the maze to close in around him again.

Plus, he was starting to feel a little like a lost kid himself.

He kept walking.

Okay, that kid is in here with you, so you're not all alone. He probably wandered off from the lost children tent ... which must mean you're getting close to the exit. Someone will find him.

He and Creepy Leaf Girl can find their way out together. Just keep walking!

Carter walked along. How long had he been in here? The sun looked just a little lower in the sky, and he realized he might have been unconscious longer than he thought. He started to jog slowly along the turning and twisting pathway. At each corner he had to choose which direction to go.

For the thousandth time he wished he had a cellphone; then he could just call his sister and she'd come and get him. Or at the very least he'd know what time it was.

But his mother always said, "No, not until you're thirteen." He always argued that it would come in handy if he was ever lost or late.

It was little comfort that he was SO right on both counts now.

This maze has to end sometime, doesn't it?

He slowed to a walk. And heard footsteps again. He stopped and listened carefully.

Sydney?

But it couldn't be Sydney. This time it sounded like many, many footsteps coming his way along the path. They sounded like angry footsteps, if that was possible. Almost like marching footsteps.

What could that be?

Carter ducked into the nearest part of the hedge.

Definitely not Sydney this time, either.

Suddenly a man burst through the bushes right beside him. He crashed through the branches and cursed. The man wore a red jacket with brass buttons and tight grey pants with tall black boots. A white sash criss-crossed his chest. He looked familiar, like a long-ago soldier that Carter had seen in history shows on TV.

Blood dripped off the soldier's arm, which he held tightly with his other hand. Carter saw a slash of skin and a bloody wound under the soldier's sleeve.

Carter gasped and bit his tongue, willing himself to stay invisible in the hedge. Vines curled slowly into his face and caressed his lips. He quietly tried to push them away. Part of him wanted to help the wounded soldier, but a bigger part wanted to stay hidden. The soldier took a sharp breath and looked around wildly, clutching his wounded arm. A drop of blood splashed onto the pathway at his feet.

Carter stared. He tried to keep his breathing steady and quiet. The marching footsteps were closer, and the wounded man in the red coat jumped back into the hedges. He looked right at Carter.

"Bloody blighters," he whispered, looking over his shoulder.

Carter jumped.

"Wh ... what? Sss ... orry?" Carter had never seen somebody clutching a wound before, especially not somebody dressed in an old-fashioned soldier's uniform.

Another historical performer? That's three now!

But Carter couldn't stare too long. The marching feet were louder, closer.

The wounded soldier took another sharp breath, looked around, and then dashed into the hedge across the pathway. As soon as he disappeared, the owners of the angry footsteps appeared. Ten soldiers in blue coats marched right past Carter. He held his breath.

The soldiers in blue carried GUNS. Old-fashioned guns with sharp knives on the end.

Carter gulped. The word "bayonet" whispered in his head....

What was going on? The soldier in red was really hurt. Why were these men chasing him? Where the heck was Mr. Green? Did he know that lost children and injured men were running around?

Carter forced himself to stay still and perfectly hidden until the angry marching footsteps faded away down the path.

Once the soldiers were gone, he popped his head out of the hedge. He should probably run and get the police, but how?

SNIP.

SNIP.

The bushes rustled, and a voice whispered in his ear: "Are you *scared* yet, Carter?"

CHAPTER 5

SCARED YET?

Carter burst out of the hedge onto the maze pathway, his eyes darting all around.

"Mr. Green? Come out! I want out of here!" he shouted.

Mr. Green walked out of the bushes. His garden shears poked out of the top of the deep pocket in his green smock, and he clutched them tightly with his deformed hand.

"It's just me, Carter. No need to shout." The old man stared at him.

Even his teeth look creepy! And don't *look at his thumb!*

Carter tried not to stare at the creepy thumb, but he couldn't help it. Mr. Green seemed not to notice and repeated his question.

"So are you? Scared? You certainly *look* scared." Mr. Green stared at Carter and blinked. He didn't even reach Carter's shoulder.

SNIP.

Mr. Green blinked again. Carter wasn't sure ... but it was entirely possible that the old man's *eyes* were made of wood, too. They were the colour of wood, speckled like wood, stiff and round like wood ...

NO! His eyes are not made of wood! No one has WOODEN eyes! Get a grip on yourself!

"Look! I've had enough, okay? There are at least two lost kids in here, and I've just seen grown-ups playing war or something. A wounded man was being chased around by angry soldiers with bayonets! You should do something!"

Carter's voice rose, but Mr. Green didn't answer. Carter was losing his temper, so he closed his eyes tight and opened them again.

He was alone. Mr. Green was gone.

Where did he go this *time?*

"Okay, play games if you want, Mr. Green, but as soon as I get out of here, I'm going to the police! Someone has to tell them what's going on in this place!"

The only answer was the breeze gently ruffling the bushes.

Carter took a deep breath and looked up into the sky. He was sure his mother and sister would be looking for him, worried by now. Maybe they had called the police, and soon the maze would be crawling with officers calling his name. That thought was a tiny relief. Eventually *someone* would come looking for him — there was no doubt about that. But when?

The old man liked scaring kids. How weird! Creepy Leaf Girl and the little boy both looked pretty scared. And who knows what was going on with the wounded soldier? Adults played weird games sometimes, like paintball and war re-enactments. Maybe there was a perfectly sane explanation for the soldier?

Carter jutted his chin out and felt just a little bit courageous. Mr. Green might be able to scare those other kids, but he wasn't going to scare *him*!

But there was another thought forming in Carter's head, one that was much more worrying than wounded soldiers, a lost child, or weird old men with deformed fingers.

What if he *couldn't find the exit?*

What if he ended up wandering around and around and around, every once in a while bumping into the little boy looking for his mom, or the wounded soldier, or worst of all, Creepy Leaf Girl?

The thought made Carter a little sick. He was starting to feel a little like the hamster at school who spent his entire life running along mazes built out of books.

Although, Carter told himself, the hamster found his way out. Most of the time.

Carter frowned. This whole situation was really weird. It didn't make sense.

But it was beginning to dawn on Carter that maybe … just maybe … the maze wasn't supposed to make sense.

He was about to start walking again when a shadow fell across the path. The hedges parted behind him, and someone tapped him on the back.

Sydney? Please be Sydney!

Carter swallowed and turned around …

IT WAS CREEPY LEAF GIRL!

Carter shrieked.

He wanted to run, but his feet wouldn't work!

Creepy Leaf Girl raised her arm and shuffled slowly toward him like a stiff young sapling tree.

Carter backed up against the hedge. Vines leapt and curled around his feet and his arms, holding him tight. Creepy Leaf Girl tried to speak, but her voice was choked. Her bonnet slipped back off her head, and leaves and small twigs popped out of her ears. Then more leaves curled out of her hair and sprouted along her eyebrows. Carter stiffened further into the hedge in horror.

"NO! DON'T COME ANY CLOSER!" he tried to scream, but the vines curled over his lips. He covered his face with his arm, and turned away.

PLEASE GO AWAY!

Creepy Leaf Girl came closer and closer, opening her arms. She opened her mouth and green, lush leaves popped out, curling over her lips, then down her long, white neck. Her voice came out in a garbled, leafy whisper, "H-e-l-p … m-e … p-l-e-a-s-e … g-a-r-d-e-n … s-h-e-a-r-s …"

Carter opened his mouth to SCREAM himself to death …

… when a strong hand yanked him backward through the hedge.

CHAPTER 6

AMAZED

Carter didn't stop to see who had grabbed him. He ran, panicked. He crashed along the pathway, stumbling over uneven bricks and past scratchy bushes. Vines leapt out of the hedge, clutching at his feet and hands. He ripped them off and kept running.

Where's Sydney! Where's the way out! Help! HELP!

He ran the pathway, dodging left and right at each turn, until he thought his heart would burst. It took him a while to realize that someone was running beside him, someone fast and strong.

Carter screwed up his courage and peeked over his shoulder. A boy about his own age ran with him. The boy smiled and then leapt past, almost leaving Carter behind.

Carter followed as fast as he could, but there was no way he could keep up. Carter wasn't a bad runner. In fact, he was a GOOD runner, but this boy was amazing.

The boy was bare-chested, and long, black hair danced down his back as he ran. He wore leather pants and moccasins on his feet.

Maybe they helped him run fast? Carter thought about all the expensive running shoes he had begged his mother for over the years and wondered briefly if maybe this boy knew something he didn't. At every turn in the pathway, the boy looked back and made sure Carter was still following.

I hope he knows the way out!

They ran for another minute, but soon Carter couldn't catch his breath. He finally stopped running at a bend in the maze and held up his hand, groaning, bent over.

"Stop! I can't run anymore," he gasped. The boy stopped, waiting, wary, watching the bushes all around them. A leather necklace with a big white claw dangled over the boy's bare chest.

A Native boy? Another historical performer? Where are all these people coming from?

"Um, hi. I'm Carter. Thanks for saving me back there. That ... that girl with the leaves. I ... I don't know how anyone can be so creepy! Do you know the way out? I'm supposed to meet my mom and my sister at the parking lot. Do you know where that is? The parking lot?" Carter slowly regained his breath.

The boy stopped smiling. He said, very slowly and carefully, like he was trying to say it perfectly, "Par ... king ... law ... t?"

"Yeah, it's over there somewhere. I think," Carter said, pointing to where he figured the maze must end.

If there WAS an end. *Please, please let there be an end.*

The boy frowned, like he didn't understand. Maybe he wasn't from around here?

"I'm Carter. CARTER."

The boy repeated very slowly, "Car ... tair."

This kid must be French or something? If he's a historical performer, he's a really good actor.

"Yeah, close enough. I've seen a lost kid, and a wounded soldier, and now that leaf girl, twice. And let's not even mention Mr. Green and his garden shears. I really just want to find the exit and go home. Do you know the way out of here? Can we go that way?" Carter pointed toward where he thought ... hoped ... his mother and sister were waiting for him.

The boy grew serious. He shook his head and cut the air with his hand across his chest. He could only be saying "NO!"

"Okay, okay! Not that way, I get it. But *do* you know the way out?" Carter asked hopefully. Finally, here was someone who seemed, well maybe not exactly normal, but possibly able to help him. Someone who could see him and understand him, sort of. Carter needed all the help he could get.

SNIP!

SNIP!

Mr. Green! The boy grabbed Carter, and they ran through the maze, dodging left and right at top speed like two silent shadows.

SNIP!

SNIP!

Wherever Mr. Green was, the Native boy seemed to stay one step ahead of him, dodging and darting along the path.

They ran until Carter was ready to collapse ... then suddenly stopped. The boy put his hands to his lips in a *shhhh* … and they listened to the breeze.

Nothing.

Nothing.

Carter strained his ears for the dreaded SNIP! SNIP! But instead he heard …

… a distant shriek! Sounds of the midway! Carter's heart pounded.

The exit must be near! They must be reaching the end of the maze! Carter thought he was going to faint with relief. They crept along quickly, keeping low.

The midway sounds got louder. More people shrieked and laughed. Carter heard music and finally, he could smell … fried food and garbage!

I never thought the smell of garbage would make me so happy!

SNIP!

SNIP!

The boy gave Carter one final enormous shove, and Carter burst out of the bushes. He blinked. He was out of the maze! He was free! The sounds and smells of the fair were all around him.

"Thank you!" Carter called out, but the boy was gone. The exit to the maze looked so harmless, just a path and a few bushes.

They really ought to put a "Danger, keep out" sign here, he thought.

He turned his back on the maze. He could go and find Sydney and his mom! They could get the police to help the wounded soldier! Then he could go home and try to forget about this weird afternoon. He looked around.

Then he frowned.

Something wasn't quite right.

He turned back to the maze … and saw an old-fashioned wooden carousel spinning around and around.

Where did THAT come from?

Carter blinked and looked again. The carousel spun and wheezed …

… but the curious maze was gone.

CHAPTER 7

THE GRAND FAIR

Carter stared. The wooden carousel went around and around. Children rode the painted wooden horses, laughing and having fun.

It didn't make sense.

Where did the maze go?

He opened and closed his eyes a few times, but the maze didn't reappear.

What? What's ... going on?

The children on the carousel all wore the same old-fashioned clothes as the little boy from the maze, and Creepy Leaf Girl.

Okay, so the maze has gone, I'm not sure how they did that, but okay. Great trick.

Magicians do make big things disappear, I think. This old-fashioned carousel is really authentic, so are the children, but at least now I know where that little boy and Creepy Leaf Girl came from. That still doesn't explain the soldier ... or the Native boy ...

Carter was a reasonable boy, trying to make reasonable sense of the situation.

But nothing really made sense. He stared at the carousel a little longer, then called out, "Pretty cool, Mr. Green! A disappearing maze, not bad, not bad at all." No one answered him, though, and the carousel riders shrieked louder than ever. The music wheezed on.

Then he remembered what Mr. Green had said when he first entered the maze: *it's the most* interesting *ride at the fair.*

The maze *was* interesting, that's for sure.

And creepy, he thought. *Be honest, it was scary, too.*

But he hadn't *really* been scared ... had he?

It didn't matter anyway, now that he was free. If Mr. Green had done something weird by somehow making the curious maze disappear, what did he care now he was out of it? If he ever saw that Native boy again, he'd have to thank him for getting him out of there. He turned to go. His mother and Sydney and the parking lot weren't far away now. He took a step, turned around a few more times, and then stopped and frowned again.

Something else was definitely not right.

Not only was the maze gone, but there was also something wrong with the midway. He'd been so happy to get out of the maze and to hear shrieks of riders and smell fried food (and garbage) that he hadn't really LOOKED at the fairgrounds.

The midway wasn't right. Not right at all.

A small wooden Ferris wheel circled up and down.

I've never seen that *there before.*

Nearby, a tiny wooden roller coaster rolled around a short track. People on the ride shrieked, but it was the least scary-looking ride Carter had ever seen, as though it was for really young kids. A large sign above it said, "Ride the Switchback! Just like Coney Island!"

Coney Island? What's that?

He heard a yell from overhead and looked up. A man in a sling rolled slowly past on a cable, as though he was zip-lining but very, very slowly. A nearby sign read: "Take your chance on the Aerial Railway!"

I've never noticed the Aerial Railway there before, either.

People flowed all around Carter as though he wasn't there. He turned in circles, his mouth open.

Where's the real midway?

Where was the mighty Double Helix Death-Defying roller coaster? And the Monster Loop-the-Loop? And the Zippedy Spinner? And the Skull-N-Bonz Pirate Ship? He'd even be happy to see the sad, so-not-scary haunted house right about now.

There were at least a dozen more rides that Carter could name that SHOULD have been on the midway, rattling on enormous wheels and making lots of noise.

But they weren't there.

Instead there was a wooden carousel, a small Ferris wheel, a tiny roller coaster, and something that looked like zip-lining with all the fun taken out.

A man walked by, shouting into an old-fashioned megaphone: "Hurry, hurry, hurry! Step right up! The grandstand horse races are about to begin!"

Horse races?

Carter ran up to him. "Hey, sir. What

happened to the midway?" he asked. But the man seemed not to hear him and kept walking. Musicians strolled past, playing guitars and drums, and more men walked by yelling strange messages into megaphones:

"Come see Bert Bostock's Leopards!" yelled one man.

"Don't miss the Mighty Swordfish in the world's largest tank!" yelled another.

"The sideshow freaks are about to perform!" bellowed a third.

There were definitely more megaphones than he remembered. And that wasn't all that was strange.

I've never seen leopards, a swordfish, or ... sideshow freaks here before!

Carter's head buzzed as he joined a huge crowd. Overhead, a bright red hot-air balloon floated in the afternoon sky. A sign on the side of the balloon said, "Watch the Daredevil Professor Stewart Soar into the Heavens!"

What's going on? What's so exciting about a hot-air balloon? The air show should start soon ... with helicopters and jets.

Carter took a deep breath, closed his eyes, and opened them again. Nothing had changed. Everything was still wrong, very, very wrong.

He spun in a slow circle. It was dawning on him that there were horses everywhere. Horses pulled buggies, carts, even big trucks. One horse-drawn truck went past, with the words ICE ICE ICE painted on the side. Carter walked up to a horse waiting patiently tied to a post and cautiously reached out to stroke its nose. The animal sniffed his hand and then stomped its front legs hard in the dirt and reared away, frightened. Carter hurried off into the crowd.

Everyone was dressed in old-fashioned clothes, not just the children on the carousel. The ladies ALL wore long dresses and fancy hats, and the men wore dark suits and hats, too.

So many hats everywhere! Even the children wore soft caps and bonnets. *Who wears so many hats?*

Carter took a few more steps. He steadied himself; he did *not* want to faint. Not here, wherever here was, and not now.

What was going on?

Food. That would help. If he was going to face something weird, at least he didn't have to face it on an empty stomach. It felt like ages since he had eaten anything.

He walked carefully past the strange midway and stepped up to a food tent. It said "Try our ICE CREAM! Guaranteed Frozen!" Beside that a sign said, "Coney Island Sausages Here! Five cents!"

Coney Island again. He had no idea what that was, but "sausage" he understood.

"Excuse me, sir, one Coney Island Sausage, please." The man ignored him, like he hadn't heard.

Carter repeated his request, louder this time. "EXCUSE ME! One sausage, please!" But the man ignored him again. Carter was just about to shout when a boy ran up to the food counter.

"One ice cream, please," the boy said.

"Of course, young man! You want to taste the best ice cream in town! That'll be five cents." The man turned to a wooden box at his feet. He removed the tight-fitting lid, and inside Carter saw a box of ice cream packed into straw-covered ice. The man scooped ice cream into a piece of waxed paper shaped like a cup and handed it to the boy.

"Don't you have an ice cream cone?" Carter asked. But the man paid no attention to him, just as though he was invisible.

When the boy had gone, the man re-opened the box lid.

"It's too hot today! This ice cream is getting soft. I need more ice," he muttered to himself. "Maybe more straw will help." The man pulled a bale of straw out from under the stall and packed a few handfuls around the block of ice.

"Why don't you just put the ice cream in the ..." The word "freezer" died on Carter's lips.

No. There wouldn't be a refrigerator with a freezer, would there? He didn't want to think about why.

Why, Carter, why doesn't he have a freezer for his ice cream?

Carter shook his head. He didn't want to answer himself.

Just then a lady walked by, holding a man's arm. She said, "Oh dear, George, the motor vehicles at the grandstand are so loud! They're far too noisy, and very dirty. I certainly hope they never catch on here. I'll take a horse and buggy every time, thank you!"

Carter clapped his hands over his ears. *NO! I did NOT just hear that lady say that!*

He opened and closed his eyes again, but nothing helped. He tried to focus on something further away. He suddenly noticed a banner that hung near the entrance to the midway: "Welcome to the Grand Fair, 1903."

Carter could feel a horrible shriek starting in his throat. His head swam.... There WERE no cars, only horses and buggies. There were NO airplanes overhead, just a hot-air balloon. There were NO huge midway rides, just small wooden ones. It was normal for people to wear old-fashioned clothes and eat food kept cold on ice.

Because it was 1903!

Carter gulped and slowly turned to the east, to the city where the huge buildings should be ... but weren't.

There were no skyscrapers, no big bank buildings. There was no modern downtown. Instead there were just small brick buildings and lots of chimneys.

Where did the city go?

Carter was definitely awake, whatever was happening. Hallucinations? Visions brought on by terror? Time travel?

But that's not possible, is it?

The lake was still there, and the big grey rock was still there too, he could see them over the food tents. So he was in the same place on the fairgrounds. He hadn't gone any*where*.

Just any *when*.

How do I get home now?

He tried not to panic. He gulped hard as his heart raced and his mouth went dry. He looked past more tents selling ice cream (guaranteed frozen!) and Coney Island sausages for five cents ...

... and saw a splotch of red squid hat disappear behind a tree.

CHAPTER 8

ARTHUR AND THE FREAK SHOW

"**S**YDNEY! SYDNEY, WAIT!"
Carter tore through the crowd. When he got to the spot where he'd seen Sydney's hat, she was gone.

"SYDNEY! SYDNEY!" He whipped around in circles. He ran from spot to spot. But there was no sign of her.

Sydney had vanished.

With a groan, Carter slid to the soft ground under a huge old tree. People and horses passed by him. Mothers, fathers, children, walked past in their best clothes, just another normal day for them, and all so terribly, terribly wrong for Carter.

No doubt about it now. This was real. No one could see him except maybe horses; he knew that now, too. He was invisible. The man with the megaphone, the Coney Island sausage man, the people all around him, none of them could see him. It was just as though he wasn't there.

Maybe no one would ever find him, either. But his sister was out there too, somewhere. That thought calmed Carter just a little. If he'd been just a little younger, he might have started crying. But instead he swallowed hard and tried to be calm.

Think, Carter, think!

He had to find his way home somehow. But how?

Where was Mr. Green?

Carter pulled his knees up to his chest. He read a sign across the grass: "FREAK SHOW." At that moment a man in a top hat came out of a big tent and yelled into a megaphone: "Step right up, ladies and gentlemen! For just ten cents, yes that's one slim dime, you can see the amazing sideshow freaks! Meet Thumbelina, the world's smallest mother! She plays guitar! See the one and only Wild Man of Borneo! He eats raw meat! And barks! And you wouldn't want to miss the bearded lady, would you? We call her Harriet, or Hairy for short!"

The crowd laughed, and then to Carter's amazement people rushed to get inside the tent. He could hear the *clink clink* as men, women, and children eagerly dropped their money into a jar at the man's feet.

A girl and her brother, two children about the same age as Carter and Sydney, pushed passed him. The girl said, "Hurry, Henry! The sideshow freaks are performing!"

Sideshow freaks? Hey, look over here! Freak boy from the future lost in time, ten cents a peek!

No one knew that a boy in strange rubber-soled shoes and oddly zippered clothes was sitting under a tree.

Was he scared? If he had to admit it … yes. If he wasn't scared before in the maze, now he was.

He *was* scared.

How was he going to get home now? Where was Mr. Green?

And where was Sydney?

He was about to get up to retrace his steps back to the carousel. He was trying very, very hard not to panic.

Then …

… "Mummy?"

A little boy stood in front of him. Could it be the boy from the maze? It was hard to tell, since all the children were dressed the same way, but he looked like the same boy.

"Hey, kid! Hey, can you see me?" Carter asked, a little frantically.

The little boy stared at him. "Mummy?" he asked again, doubtful. But he was definitely looking at Carter. The little boy could see him, he was sure of it.

"Kid … listen carefully. Where's the maze?" The little boy stuck his finger in his nose and frowned.

"Lost my mummy," he said again, a little fearful. Carter grabbed the boy's shoulder. He was real enough.

"Where's your mom? Back in the maze? Where is it? Where's the maze, kid?" Carter wanted to shake him, so he forced himself to calm down. But the little boy just stared. His big eyes filled with tears. Carter sighed and took the boy's hand (the one that *hadn't* just been in his nose).

"What's your name?"

"Arthur."

"Okay, Arthur. Come on, let's go and find your mom," he said. If he couldn't find the maze, and he couldn't help himself, at least he could help this little lost boy find his mother.

It felt better, much, much better, having someone see him and speak to him, even if it was just a lost five-year-old.

"Mummy?"

"No, Arthur, I'm not your mom, sorry. We're both lost," Carter said.

"No! Look!" the little boy said, more urgently this time. He was pointing at something.

SNIP!

SNIP!

Mr. Green!

CHAPTER 9

THE WILD MAN OF BORNEO

"HEY! MR. GREEN! STOP!" Carter yelled. Mr. Green vanished into a building with the word "Horses" carved into the marble arch over the door.

Carter tore through the crowd but screeched to a halt. A little voice wailed behind him, "Mummy!" When Carter looked back, Arthur was running after him, crying.

"Come on, Arthur!" Carter grabbed the boy's pudgy fist. "Mr. Green is in here!"

The boys ran into the enormous building filled with weird displays and packed with people. Carter stopped, frantically looking for Mr. Green. Straw littered the floor, and stable boys with wooden boxes and shovels ran around cleaning up after horses tied to posts. There were steaming piles of manure everywhere. Giant flies were abundant.

How does anyone keep clean in 1903? Carter wondered, sidestepping a large pile of horse poo. The place smelled of leather, straw, and animals. And manure. Definitely manure.

A big crowd of men stood around an old-fashioned tractor with big metal wheels. It had a sign on it: "See the amazing Avery Traction Truck! Does the work of fifty horses!"

Carter pushed through the huge crowd and stood on his tiptoes, straining to see over the hats on many, many heads. There were so many people, so many hats, that he couldn't see very far. He pushed and pushed, dragging the little boy with him.

First they struggled past an enormous beer bottle that went from the floor to the ceiling.

That's a LOT of beer!

Then they pushed past a huge tub of something called "MacLaren's Imperial Cheese." Women in long dresses and feathered hats stood tasting the cheese in tiny spoonfuls.

That's a LOT of cheese, too! It'll take them forever to eat it all!

They carried on, running past a life-sized statue of a lion carved out of soap. The place was just getting weirder and weirder. Carter felt like he'd gotten stuck in some land designed for giants.

SNIP.

SNIP.

Carter spun around. He craned his neck around the ladies' hats and the towers of cheese and soap …

… and there! Mr. Green!

"STOP! MR. GREEN!" The old man was fast!

Carter pushed people aside, skidding to a halt out the back door. He looked around, frantic.

Where was he? Where was Mr. Green?

There!

A green smock swirled through a nearby tent flap. Carter and Arthur followed fast, and ran into the tent past a man wearing a top hat. The man tried to grab Arthur but the little boy dodged just in time.

"Stop! You there, boy! You owe me ten cents! Stop, thief!"

But the boys kept running and melted into the huge crowd inside the dark, stuffy tent. They skidded to a halt in a crowd of people staring at a man in a cage.

He wore a leopard-skin robe.

And he was barking.

Carter did a double take. Other than the barking and the leopard skin robe, the man looked totally normal and possibly a little bored. The sign attached to his cage said, "The Wild Man of Borneo."

He looks like he's in a zoo!

No time to stare. He grabbed Arthur, and they elbowed past more people.

"Do you see Mr. Green?" Carter whispered.

A shout made Carter jump. The man in the top hat scanned the dark tent for Arthur. The crowd was big, but not big enough to hide them for long.

"This way!" Carter whispered. The boys hurried past a tiny lady sitting on a stool, holding a small guitar. The woman smiled. The sign beside her chair said, "Meet Thumbelina, the world's smallest mother."

"Are you lost, little boy?" she asked. Carter tried to pull him away, but Arthur wouldn't budge.

"Have you seen my mummy?" the little boy asked. The crowd was parting, and the top hat got closer and closer in the darkness. They had to go!

"No, I'm afraid not. But if you're looking for that man with the green smock and the garden shears, he went that way, dear," Thumbelina whispered, pointing.

"Thank you!"

"You're welcome," she said pleasantly.

The man in the top hat searched through the crowd, getting closer and closer. Another lady across the tent smiled and jerked her head, making her long beard wobble. Carter tried not to shout in surprise. "Over there ..." the bearded lady whispered.

"HEY! YOU THERE! STOP THIEF!" The man in the top hat was upon them! But Carter and Arthur had already seen a green smock swirl through a spear of sunshine at the back of the tent.

SNIP!

SNIP!

The man in the top hat took an enormous swipe at Arthur, but the boys dodged him and burst out of the tent into the sunshine after Mr. Green ...

... and skidded to a halt.

"Where's Mummy?" the little boy asked, puzzled. .

They stood in tall grass, facing the lake. Beside them was the big grey rock. But the sideshow tent, the bearded lady, Thumbelina, the man in the top hat, the crowd gawking at the Wild Man of Borneo, the horses, the midway, Mr. Green ... were gone.

Everything was gone.

The Grand Fair 1903 had vanished.

CHAPTER 10

BATTLEFIELD

Carter stared in disbelief. For a second, he thought he heard a very faint sound of people on a midway. Then silence. He ran back to where the sideshow tent should have been and waved his arms around, but it was no use.

Everything that had been there a moment before had vanished.

Instead, there was grass, lake, and the big grey rock. Carter was glad the rock was still there, the one that he and Sydney had eaten ice cream beside before this weird afternoon began. At least something was still the same.

But there was no sign of Mr. Green. Or Sydney. Or the sideshow tent.

Carter took a huge breath of fresh air. No smell of garbage, no fried food — not even any horse manure.

Okay, so the fair in 1903 has disappeared, just like the maze. What now?

And when?

Carter sat in the deep grass and tried to clear his swirling head. What was going on here? He felt slightly sick. Arthur stood in front of him and rubbed his eyes, a chubby little reminder of 1903. Carter didn't feel so well. Time travel, hallucinations, a weirdly real dream? Whatever this was, it was making him feel very, very strange.

He tried to focus. Whatever was happening, they had no choice but to go forward.

"Where are we now, do you think, Arthur?" Carter dug his heels into the long grass.

"I don't know." The little boy dropped into the grass beside Carter. "There are lots of trees cut down, though," he added.

Carter looked around and realized Arthur was right. Tree stumps dotted the field all around.

"There's a big forest, too," Arthur added. He was right again, since nearby a huge, towering forest stood where the stumps stopped. The forest looked like it had stood there forever, and no one had chopped it down or paved it over. It was quiet, very, very quiet. Carter could hear his own heartbeat and Arthur's breathing.

It was creepy quiet.

Carter bit his lip. "Okay, Arthur, get up on my shoulders and see if you can see anything." The little boy climbed up, and Carter turned slowly in a circle.

"People!" Arthur called out.

"Hey! You're right! There's a town!" Small wooden buildings dotted the shore in the distance, and smoke rose from far-off chimneys. A sailing ship that looked like a toy sat offshore in the bay.

Could that be ... the city? It's so tiny! It's just a little town now.

Still, it was a relief. There were people around. There was a town nearby!

Then Carter noticed more signs of life.

"Look, Arthur, there's a flag on that hill over there, and I smell smoke," Carter said. He tried to keep his voice even; he didn't want to scare the little boy too much. He didn't need a crying child on his hands on top of everything else.

He very badly wanted to shout for Mr. Green, but there was a silence to the place that made him wary. Something told him he should be careful and stay hidden. The little boy looked up at Carter, and for a moment Carter felt sorry for him. Here was a five-year-old who was lost and somehow stuck in this strange place with him.

"Alright. So, here's what I think. Somehow, we must still be on the fairgrounds ... the lake is the same. The big grey rock is still here. There's a small town way down the shoreline, where the city should be. So I think we're in the same place. I'm not sure *when* we are, though. Before skyscrapers. Before tall buildings, before even small stone buildings, I guess."

The little boy stared at Carter and blinked. Then he shivered in his coat, and Carter noticed for the first time that the afternoon had grown cold. In fact, it no longer felt like summer but more like a cool spring day. Somehow the season had changed too.

"Okay. So where there's a flag and smoke, there are people. Come on, let's go see if we can find Mr. Green. But be quiet."

He took Arthur by the hand, and they crept slowly across the field toward the smell of smoke and the fluttering flag. They kept low and hidden behind fallen trees and stumps. Which wasn't hard. Someone had cut down a LOT of trees. Some of the stumps were so huge that Carter couldn't imagine how big the tree must have been, or how old, before it got chopped down. And beyond that stood the enormous green forest. You couldn't see past the trunks, they were so thick and solidly grown together. And tall.

They crept along, down a small hill, over a shallow creek, then to the bottom of the hill below the flag. It fluttered above them on a stone wall. Small, sharpened tree trunks stuck out of the hill, right at eye level. You'd never be able to climb over them; they were good defence against anyone trying to climb the hill.

Jutting out of the wall above his head, Carter saw the round, metal nose of a huge gun.

A ... cannon?

No doubt about it. A cannon stuck out of the brick wall above his head, pointing back the way they had just come.

"Carter!" Arthur pointed above them.

Carter looked up, and the little boy was right. A man stood on the wall above their heads. He wore grey pants, a red jacket, and he carried a long gun with a pointed end. A bayonet! Carter pulled the little boy down into the grass beside him.

"A soldier!" Carter whispered. As he watched, more men in grey pants and red coats stood on the wall above them. They carried bayonets that glinted in the sunlight.

Then a loud voice shouted: "Rally, men! The enemy is near! Ready the twenty-four-pounder! Prepare to fire!"

Carter gasped. *The enemy is near? Wasn't there a battle around here a long time ago, during a war?*

He and Arthur were sitting right below a cannon....

"COME ON, ARTHUR!" Carter dragged the little boy away from the bottom of the hill, away from the dark snout of the gigantic gun.

KA-BOOOOOM! KA-BOOOOOOOM!

Both boys fell into the grass. Rocks and stones rained down while Arthur wailed and covered his ears. Carter gasped and grabbed the little boy, wrapping his arms around him.

JEEEEZZ! I'll never be able to hear properly again! Carter peeked up at the cannon. Smoke furled out of the gun like a dragon's snout. He could see the soldiers in red coats pouring more black powder into the back end of the enormous gun.

"Come on!" Carter clutched the little boy's hand and dragged him to a nearby hill.

Arthur bravely bit his lip, but his eyes shone with tears. The soldiers on the wall shouted. The stinging smoke from the cannon hurt Carter's eyes. He did NOT want to be so close to it when it fired a second time.

Now that they were farther up the hill, Carter could see more clearly. They were hiding near a handful of wooden buildings, and soldiers in red coats ran from building to building with guns and long swords.

More shrieks and shouts.

KA-BOOOOOM! KA-BOOOOOOOM!

The earth shook again, the trees wobbled, the windows in the wooden building in front of them rattled.

Now I know what cannon-fire sounds like, I hope I never hear it again!

Inside the fort, frantic soldiers ran through doorways and down steep stone steps, carrying guns, swords, hatchets, and barrels of gunpowder. More soldiers whizzed by in a blur of red jackets.

Carter watched the soldiers closely, then Arthur grabbed him and pointed at the forest.

"Look, Carter," he whimpered.

Soldiers in blue coats crept through the woods. The enemy! What should he do? No one could see him, so he couldn't warn the soldiers. He'd never felt so helpless!

But whatever Carter did wouldn't have mattered because then …

… it was *war*.

With a shout, the soldiers on the wall saw the enemy creeping through the woods. Guns fired. Musket balls whined overhead. Men shrieked. Thick white smoke filled the air. Native warriors with guns and knives ran from the woods, and soldiers in red coats tore down the hill to join them in the fight against the enemy.

Then the madness really started.

Soldiers in blue coats and soldiers in red coats ran at each other across the field of stumps. Swords flashed, then clashed. Gunshots fired. Men screamed and yelled. Within a few seconds, the air was thick with white smoke that choked Carter's throat and burned his eyes. The shiny tips of bayonets sliced the air, and it was impossible to see anything in the mayhem.

But worse than that was the noise.

Screams, shouts, gunshots, running feet, more shouts, more gunshots. Groans of injured men. Carter realized he had forgotten to breathe for a few moments, he'd been holding his breath so hard.

Arthur whimpered and hid his face in Carter's shoulder. Carter put his arm around the little boy. The two boys huddled behind the wooden building, as far from the bullets and screams as they could get, but they were far from safe.

What should we do? How are we going to get out of this? I'm too scared to get up!

BANNNNGGG! A gunshot went off right beside Carter's ear. He'd never be able to hear again! Thick white smoke filled his face, and the singe of gunpowder filled his nostrils.

A second later a wounded soldier in a red coat ran past, gripping his arm. A drop of blood splashed over his feet. He ran by their hiding spot, looked right at Carter and cried out, "Bloody blighters!" The soldier dashed away, chased by ten blue-coated soldiers who loomed out of the smoke. Their bayonets bristled like tree trunks, sharp and deadly.

"I saw them in the maze!" Carter whispered. First Arthur in 1903, and now the wounded soldier … what could it mean?

Then …

SNIP!

SNIP!

Carter jumped up from his hiding spot.

There! Mr. Green! A green smock swirled around the side of a wooden building across the grassy fort. Carter was about to call out, to run and follow Mr. Green.

But then suddenly another sound caught

his ear very, very faintly, so faintly that he almost missed the familiar voice: *Carter! Carter!*

It was SYDNEY!

No mistaking it this time: past the smoke and madness on the battlefield below, a tiny red hat bobbed along.

Sydney was calling him from the edge of the forest.

CHAPTER 11

THE GRAND MAGAZINE

"**S**YDNEY!" Carter screamed. He waved his arms and yelled. He didn't care if there was a battle raging all around him. He screamed his sister's name again, but as soon as he saw her at the edge of woods, she disappeared.

He fell into the grass and put his head in his hands. He really, really wanted to cry, but he couldn't, not now and not in front of Arthur. He felt a little hand take his, and a small voice said, "It's okay, Carter. I saw my mummy too. Or I thought I did."

Carter snapped his head up. "What? What

do you mean? You saw your mom?" Arthur's soft eyes filled with tears.

"I … I just thought I saw her too. Down there. I heard her call me. It happened before."

Carter stared at the little tear-stained face. A strange possibility was slowly occurring to him. "Arthur … do you think Sydney and your mom are calling us from the future, from the maze? And we can hear them, through some trick of the maze? Or some trick of Mr. Green?"

Arthur looked confused, so Carter went on, more sure that he was right.

"I mean, do you think it's possible that we're still in the maze somehow?"

Arthur looked doubtful and then shrugged. "Maybe. I miss Mummy," he said and closed his eyes. Looking at the small boy, Carter suddenly remembered what it was like to be little and scared. The haunted house used to scare him. What must it be like for poor Arthur, stuck here somewhere *really* scary, not just pretend scary?

"You can't sleep now, buddy. Let's go."

It was now very clear to Carter what they had to do. He was remembering something that Mr. Green had said in the maze: *Every maze is a journey. You just have to choose the right path.* Carter had to choose now. Who to follow? Sydney was down in the forest, or a future version of her was somehow still in the maze. Arthur's mom was down there too, calling her son. Mr. Green was behind them in the fort, but in the past few moments Carter had noticed soldiers frantically running in and out of a wooden building with the words "Grand Magazine" hanging over the door.

He didn't know what a grand magazine was, exactly, but it didn't sound good. And he'd just heard one of the soldiers shout they were ready to "blow the magazine." Whatever "magazine" meant in this time period, he was pretty sure it wasn't something to read, and grand could only be big. Plus the only thing you could "blow" up, as far as he knew, was gunpowder. They had to get out of there, and *fast*.

He looked down at Arthur. If they ran for the woods, could the little boy keep up?

Carter suddenly wished this was all just a scary, weird, super-long dream. Perhaps he'd wake up when it was all over. But a little hand clutched his too tightly for it to be a dream. It hurt. The screams and shouts and noise of battle were too real for him to be sleeping or hallucinating. Not to mention the mind-numbing cannon. His ears would probably ring forever.

He took a deep breath and whispered in Arthur's ear. "We have to be really brave. They're blowing up the Grand Magazine, and that can't be good, whatever it means. I don't want to be here when they do. Plus Sydney's out there calling from the maze somehow. And your mom too. Mr. Green is behind us in the fort somewhere … but that Native boy didn't follow him in the maze, and he found the exit. We have to choose who to follow … and I choose Sydney and your mom. Agreed?"

The little boy solemnly nodded.

"Okay. Can you run really fast, like you did in the sideshow tent?"

Arthur nodded again.

The battle raged even further from the trees. It was now or never. With his heart in his mouth, Carter did the bravest thing he'd ever done: he clasped Arthur by the hand, and together the two boys slipped down the grassy hill and ran away from the soldiers' fort. And away from Mr. Green.

I CANNOT believe I'm doing this … I do NOT want to run across a battlefield!

They slid down the hill into the thick smoke and mayhem. Carter ran as fast as he could toward the forest, half-dragging the little boy at his side. The sounds of the wounded soldiers, the shrieks of warriors, and clash of swords threatened to stop him, but he charged on.

I really don't want to see any more wounded soldiers!

The air was so thick with smoke, it was hard to see. The boys ran and stumbled across the grass toward the trees. For a horrifying second, a blue-coated soldier loomed toward them out of the smoke, but the boys dodged him and ran on, almost at the trees, almost at safety …

… THWANGGGG! An axe whizzed right past Carter's ear and stuck in a tree beside his head. Arthur gasped.

"Run, Arthur!" Carter screamed, shoving the little boy the last few steps into the forest.

Carter! Carter!

There! There in the distant gloom of the forest … a tiny speck of red!

Sydney's hat!

With a final, powerful leap and an energy he didn't know he had, Carter dragged Arthur into the dark woods …

… just as the grand magazine blew the fort and the world to pieces behind them.

CHAPTER 12

CLAMS AND EAGLES

The silence hurt Carter's ears. He slowly opened his eyes and saw Arthur sleeping peacefully on the ground beside him.

He was lying on a soft bed of pine needles, looking up, up, up into the tallest trees he'd ever seen. The air was clean and fresh, and the woods were silent, silent. He could hear water nearby. He rolled onto his side and looked at Arthur.

Peaceful as a baby, fast asleep.

Then he remembered. Battle cries, smoke, gunshots. An explosion. A fireball behind them. Running further into the forest to escape the heat and fire. Then nothing. He and Arthur had survived the explosion of the fort and the grand magazine, although Carter knew that plenty of soldiers hadn't. He tried not to think about that. He had to focus.

Where were they now?

Carter looked around. The sun shone weakly, struggling through a canopy of trees high above. It was dark where they lay, very dark and still.

And it was QUIET. He strained his ears, but the only sound was the gentle lapping of water against the shore.

He looked through the trees and saw the lake.

"Come on, sleepyhead, time to wake up," Carter said gently, prodding the little boy. "We have to find out where we are now. Or … when, I guess."

Arthur woke up slowly and smiled at Carter. Then he stood up and took Carter's hand. He looked no worse for wear after their ordeal on the battlefield, although somewhere along the way Arthur had lost his cap.

They walked out of the forest to the lake. It hadn't changed much, except now the trees marched right down to the shoreline. No stumps. No one had been there to cut down the trees, yet.

And the huge grey rock was still there beside the water.

What a relief! Carter had the weirdest impulse to run over and hug it, since it was the only thing that he could count on. In this long, strange afternoon, it hadn't failed him. Mr. Green, Sydney, even time itself came and went, but the rock was as big and solid as ever.

Carter scanned the distance. The soldiers' fort was definitely gone. The bay was the same, except this time there was no tiny wooden city off in the distance, no wooden ship with sails full in the bay, no flags fluttering nearby, no smoke. Just trees, trees, trees, and water.

And silence.

It was very, very eerie.

It looked like the kind of place that no one had visited.

Ever.

Suddenly Arthur let out a happy cry and ran into the water, giggling and splashing.

Carter couldn't help it. He smiled. It WAS hot and buggy. It felt like high summer again, no longer a cool spring day. He sat in the shade of the rock, as he had done with Sydney back when the world was still normal and frozen ice cream existed. When was that, exactly?

Hours before? Centuries in the future? He had a headache and his ears were ringing, which he sincerely hoped was a temporary effect of time travel and not permanent hearing damage from the grand magazine explosion.

He watched Arthur play in the water and scanned the shoreline. He strained his ears for any sound: Sydney calling his name, or even the dreaded SNIP! SNIP!

But all was silent.

Little silver fish darted in the shallows, and fresh-water clams crowded the shore.

When was the last time there were clams in the city harbour? Arthur took a huge drink of lake water, scooping it in his hands. Carter was about to stop him but then realized he didn't have to. The water was clean enough to drink. No one, not even crazy people, would drink the water in the harbour in Carter's time.

He scanned the shore, the trees, and tried to concentrate.

Think, Carter! You have to get home. You have to get Arthur home, too.

Arthur skipped rocks for a while. Then he tossed a stick out into the water and threw rocks at it. He hit the stick, every time.

A huge bird flew overhead, and Carter

watched it soar. An eagle! An EAGLE flew overhead on the shores of the lake beside his city!

When was the last time an eagle lived here? Hundreds of years ago, for sure.

What are we going to do? We can't leave this spot. We're where we're supposed to be, just not when. There has to be a way home. There's a way out of every maze. Even the hamster at school knows that. But where's Mr. Green?

The only sound was the hum of bugs, and the tick! tick! as Arthur threw rocks at the stick in the water. Carter wanted to call out for Mr. Green, for Sydney, for anybody, but there was a quietness to this place that made him whisper. Who knew what was out there in the dark forest?

At least there aren't any dinosaurs around. Probably.

Carter reached down to pick up a stick … and saw a movement at the edge of the beach.

"Arthur, come here," he whispered. The little boy whirled around and looked at Carter, then turned to look where Carter was trying NOT to look. The two boys stared down the beach, and Carter bit his tongue. He willed Arthur not to scream.

A huge bear lumbered out of the forest, sniffed the air … and looked right at them.

CHAPTER 13

CAR-TAIR!

"Come here!" Carter hissed, peeking around the side of the boulder. Arthur slipped across the beach.

"*A bear!*"

"I know, shhhh." Carter gulped and sweat poured down his back. His heart was pounding so hard, he was seriously worried that it was going to burst.

Go away, stupid bear!

Carter peeked around the edge of the boulder again and bit his tongue. The bear hadn't moved but was on its hind legs now, looking their way, sniffing the air.

Okay, THINK! We can't outrun it. We can't get to the trees fast enough to hide, and it'll see us, anyway. We could run into the water ... bears can swim, though, I think. Probably faster than me and definitely faster than Arthur. We could ... climb on top of the boulder, but that's not very far above the bear's head. It would just climb up and eat us. Maybe not, though ... the rock is tall. And round. Maybe the bear can't climb it?

THINK Carter, THINK!

Carter peeked around the corner of the boulder again. He almost cried out.

The bear was coming.

Carter took a huge breath. He was NOT going to die here beside the lake in some past time. He'd been through too much already today. If a grand magazine explosion wasn't enough to kill him, then NO WAY was a bear going to eat him. It just wasn't going to happen. He wasn't going to LET it happen. His mother and his sister were waiting for him in his own time, and Arthur's mom was waiting for him too, in 1903. Whatever was happening to him, he was NOT GOING TO DIE HERE! And neither was the little boy at his side.

He turned to whisper to Arthur.

"The bear's coming this way." Arthur nodded, looking with huge, tearful eyes up at Carter.

"You were brave when we ran into the sideshow tent after Mr. Green, and you were brave when we ran across the battlefield. Do you think you can be brave again?" Arthur squeezed his eyes shut, but nodded once.

"Good. We climb up the rock, okay?" Carter peered around the boulder, and his heart stopped. The bear was definitely walking toward them, slowly wagging its massive head from side to side … it would be at the boulder in moments. Sooner, if it decided to do anything but amble.

Please go away … please go away …

Carter quietly boosted Arthur up onto the boulder. It was actually pretty high, over his arms as high as he could reach. The little boy clambered up, and then it was Carter's turn. He'd never climbed a boulder before, though, it really wasn't that easy.

He managed to get halfway up then realized he wasn't going to make it in time.

The bear had seen Arthur and decided to investigate. It came at a trot, sniffing the air and snorting.

Carter could feel the weight of the bear trotting across the beach under him. He gritted his teeth, he swore, he pulled with all his might, his shirt was caught on the rock … he was almost at the top …

… when hot breath struck his leg!

STINKING BEAR BREATH!

Everything happened fast after that. With one final heave, Carter dragged himself onto the top of the boulder. Then with a heart-stopping ROARRRRR … the bear charged.

Arthur screamed, and Carter shielded him in a hug.

ROARRRR!

Horrible bear breath filled the air. Enormous curved claws raked down the rock, leaving deep scratches. There wasn't anywhere to hide. Any second now, the bear would leap onto the rock, and that would be the end …

I don't want to die here … I don't want to die here!

The bear roared in their faces, swiping at them again and again with a gigantic paw, but they were just out of reach. For a few seconds, anyway.

"Close your eyes, Arthur!" Carter whispered softly. "Just don't look!"

BANGGGGG!

A gunshot.

The bear huffed in surprise and dropped to the ground. It roared one last time and then turned and ran into the woods.

Carter let Arthur go and opened his eyes.

Out in the open water, a canoe glided by. A Native man sat in the back of the canoe, settling a long gun over his shoulder. He started paddling.

In the front of the canoe, a boy raised his hand and smiled. As the canoe glided away along the shoreline, the boy's voice carried over the water:

"Car-tair!"

CHAPTER 14

MAIS OUI!

The boy from the maze!

Carter waved and shouted, "Hey! Hey, over here! HEY!" but the canoe glided away down the beach, out of sight around a bend.

"Come on!" Carter and Arthur slid down off the rock and ran together down the beach, calling and waving. It was no use. The canoe had disappeared.

Carter watched it vanish with despair. It would be easy, so easy, to slump to the beach at that point. To just lie down and give up, to stare at the late afternoon sky. Carter considered it, he really did.

"What now, Carter?" the little boy asked, leaning his head into Carter's arm. Carter sighed. He had to go on; he couldn't stop now. Carter had finally figured it out for sure: somehow they *were* still in the maze. He'd found Arthur, the wounded soldier, and now the Native boy, all the people he'd seen in the maze. The only person missing was Creepy Leaf Girl. They just had to keep going until she turned up too, then maybe … maybe that's when this whole strange journey would end. He looked down at Arthur, who was trying very hard not to cry. What a scary day for a little kid.

"Come on, climb aboard." Carter squatted down and then piggybacked Arthur along the beach to follow the canoe, carefully picking his way through the rocks and sand.

They didn't have to go far. As they rounded a bend, they saw the empty canoe bumping gently against the beach. The man and boy were in the distance, climbing a steep, sandy bank, struggling under large bundles.

"Hey! Over here!" Carter yelled, but the pair disappeared over the top of the hill.

Carter helped Arthur up the sandy hill to follow the Native boy. It was a hard climb, and the pair struggled upward. As they neared the top …

… Carter smelled smoke.

And heard voices. A man clearly said, "Gaston! May we!"

More sounds followed: metal clanged on metal, a cow bellowed, children laughed.

What can possibly be up there?

They struggled up the hill, and … there at the top was the strangest sight! A cluster of small buildings sat in a meadow, protected by a tall wooden wall. All around the clearing, people worked, talked, laughed.

Another fort? Where the heck are we?

Carter pulled Arthur down to the grass behind a low wooden fence, and they watched. This wasn't like the fort with the cannon. This was older, smaller, and these people weren't soldiers, they were just … people.

Very busy people.

A cow was tied to a post near their hiding spot, and a young woman in a long dress and a bonnet sat on a stool and milked it. Chickens fretted in wooden cages, and another woman searched for eggs beneath them. Two small dogs ran from spot to spot, sniffing and wagging their tails. They ran over to Carter and Arthur, sniffed them, and then growled and ran off.

The sound of metal clanging was a black-smith hammering on a table in a small building. A red-hot fire burned behind him, and sweat poured down his face and neck.

But more interesting than all that to Carter were the Native men, women and children standing nearby. They were dressed like the boy from the maze, in moccasins and leather, or wore colourful shirts or neck scarves, and leather leggings. The men had guns, bows, or knives and talked with the men who weren't Natives.

Arthur slipped his hand into Carter's. This was strange, Carter had to agree. He thought they were all alone in this time, whenever this was. But here was a fort, bustling with activity and people. It wasn't big, and there weren't a *lot* of people, but it was definitely thriving.

Carter heard the words "May we" again, then suddenly realized what they were really saying: *Mais, oui!*

They were speaking French!

Carter knew the lake was still there, and the big grey rock was back down the beach, like always. So whenever they were this time, they were still on the fairgrounds. But since when did Natives and Europeans sit together speaking *French* in his city?

The boys watched, carefully quiet. Two French men sat at a long wooden table piled high with bright green, red, and blue beads, and next to that was a small pile of silver buttons, stars, and moons. Bundles of bright red material sat nearby, and four axe heads glinted in the sun.

Everyone seemed happy. Whatever was going on here, it was an exciting day.

Carter couldn't pull his eyes away. It was a late summer day in his city, and here he was, just an arm's length away from people who had lived here long before him.

French men and women.

And Natives. The first people to live in this place, the first ones to walk along the streams and forest paths that had long been buried or paved over. Eagles flew overhead, the water in the harbour was clean and clear and filled with clams, and bears roamed the forest. Never in his wildest dreams could he have imagined his city this way, or its first inhabitants standing so close to him.

It made the entire horrible afternoon seem almost … better. There were *some* benefits to time travel, maybe. It wasn't all terrifying battles and freak shows. There was this too, these

people, this interesting place and time, whatever this was.

He held his breath and watched.

What are they doing?

Carter watched closely as a Native man
dropped a bundle of dark furs on the long
wooden table. A French man measured the
height of the bundle with a wooden stick and
then passed one of the dark red blankets and a
bag of silver beads back to him.

They were trading! The Native hunters and the French men were trading animal
furs for blankets and beads. No wonder the
Native man had taken a shot at the bear from
the canoe. He hadn't seen Carter and Arthur;
he'd just seen a valuable bear fur.

Carter had never heard of a French trading
fort around there, and no one had ever men-
tioned it in history class at school.

When did this happen?

Arthur poked him. Someone was staring
at them.

The boy from the maze stood near the
adults, but he was watching Carter and
Arthur closely. Carter had been so engrossed
in watching the Natives and the traders, he'd
almost forgotten about the boy. He raised his

hand and the boy crept over, ducking down to their hiding spot.

"Car-tair," he said quietly. Not a question, just a hello.

"It's you! You saved me from the maze, and your father saved us from the bear! Thank you! Do you think you could save me one last time? I need to find Mr. Green? The old guy, SNIP, SNIP ... you know? SNIP, SNIP?"

The boy frowned, but Carter tried again. "Look, I'm exhausted and I have to get this little guy home. I want to go home, too. Believe it or not, I've been in three different time periods today, I've seen a LOT of weird stuff. You don't seem too surprised to see me, though, so maybe this has happened before? Maybe you see people from the maze all the time? It's been an interesting afternoon, but right now I just want to go home!" On the word "home," Carter's voice wobbled, just a bit.

Yes, he wanted to go home. Was that too much to ask? He'd almost forgotten what home was like, he'd seen so much in the past few hours.

The boy looked over his shoulder at his father, who was deep in conversation with one of the traders. The boy looked back at Carter, then nodded. He looked over at his father one more time then ducked and crept past his parent's careful eye toward the forest.

Carter and Arthur followed. They snuck past a wooden house filled with sacks and boxes, then past a sheep pen, then past a small garden and something that definitely smelled like an outhouse. They crept outside the fort gates, then past a tiny patch of wooden crosses.

A cemetery. Definitely the oldest cemetery in the city!

Then they were at the very edge of the dark green forest. The boy pointed into the deep woods and said, "SNIP, SNIP."

Carter gulped. The sun was low in the sky, barely piercing the treetops. The sounds of the fort were already far away, and the last thing Carter wanted to do was enter the dark green forest just as night fell.

But there could be no mistaking the Native boy. He pointed into the deep woods again and repeated those two words that Carter had come to dread: "SNIP, SNIP."

Carter took a deep breath and nodded. "Okay, I get it, Mr. Green is in there. Thanks, but I really don't want to do this."

The boy put his hand on Carter's shoulder and said softly, "Car-tair." His smile made

Carter brave. He could do it — he could take Arthur into the dark, terrifying woods and look for Mr. Green.

Plus Sydney was out there, too, in some future time, calling his name. And Arthur's mom.

The boy raised his hand in a final farewell then disappeared back to the fort.

"See you," Carter said quietly to his retreating back. "If you're ever in *my* time, I'll show you your city, although it's changed a little."

And hopefully you'll be braver than me.

CHAPTER 15

SUNDOWN

It was so dark that Carter almost couldn't see Arthur's face. The trees grew closer and closer together, and the late afternoon sun barely filtered down to the forest floor.

They crept along, working their way deeper into the gloom.

Suddenly Carter heard the sound of running water ahead. He *shhh'd* Arthur, and the two boys snuck over fallen logs and through the tightly growing tree trunks toward the sound.

SNIP!

SNIP!

Carter stopped.

Mr. Green stood beside a tiny, bubbling fountain. The water came up out of the ground and ran into a little stream that grew into a pool, and then meandered into the woods. Mr. Green stooped and took a drink.

"Hello, Carter," he said without looking up. "You've finally found me. It took you long enough, much longer than most children. You must have dawdled."

Dawdled?

"You! You're crazy! What have you done to us? We want to go home!"

Suddenly Carter wasn't scared. The whole afternoon flashed before him, the Wild Man of Borneo, the terrifying battlefield, the scary bear, and the constant feeling of being lost and weirdly out of place. No, he wasn't scared — all he felt was mad.

It felt good to be mad.

"You have no right to steal kids and send them back through time in your stupid maze! I don't even care how you did it ... or why ... but it's time to stop this! We're lost, we're tired, Arthur is scared ... we almost got *blown up* by a huge gunpowder explosion during a BATTLE and ... then a *bear* tried to eat us! If it wasn't for that Native boy ..."

"Ah, yes, him," the old man said. He snapped upright, and Carter was SURE he heard a cracking, like a twig. Mr. Green stared at Carter with his brown wooden eyes. Carter's own eyes were getting used to the gloom, and he suddenly noticed a girl standing perfectly still behind a tree, looking at him.

It was Creepy Leaf Girl. Finally, the last person from the maze! Carter gulped. The girl didn't have leaves growing out of her ears this time, thankfully. She just looked old-fashioned and normal. She smiled at Carter behind Mr. Green's back.

Mr. Green didn't stop talking.

"Ah yes, the Native boy. The magic of the maze is very old indeed, but his people have lived in this spot long before the maze arrived, so it holds no power over him. He was the first child to walk through the maze in this place, the first child to find his way out. He can come and go as he pleases and show others the way to me. It's annoying. Most children I choose for the maze have to work hard to find the exit, unless he's around."

"What do you mean, 'choose?' Why did you choose us?" Carter pulled Arthur closer.

"You, Carter? You were an interesting case. You were the boy who found everything dull, remember? You said, and I quote, 'Nothing interesting has ever happened around here in the history of the world.' I wonder if you think that now? And as for Arthur ... well ... you needed a sidekick, didn't you?" Mr. Green stooped to take another drink from the fountain. Behind him, Creepy Leaf Girl looked hard at something, again and again. She kept looking at whatever it was and then looking back at Carter. He followed her eyes.

Mr. Green's red-handled garden shears lay against a tree. It was only the second time that Carter had ever seen them out of the old man's hands or out of his smock pocket.

The old man talked and took sips from the bubbling fountain.

"How did you like the bear? Or the grand magazine? Or the freak show? All quite *interesting*, don't you think? Or did you find them boring, too?" On and on he went, drinking from the fountain and talking.

Creepy Leaf Girl was still telling Carter something with her eyes. She kept darting looks at the garden shears against the tree. She wanted him to do something with them.

But what?

The old man was speaking. "Did you like how only other children and animals can see you in the maze? That's always been a nice touch, I think, don't you? Very disturbing not to know who can see you ... and who can't. What do you think of time travel, Carter?" Mr. Green peered at Carter and blinked his wooden eyes. He didn't bother hiding his creepy thumb, and no doubt about it this time: leaves slowly sprouted and spiralled around his hand like an emerald green serpent.

"What? What do you want with us? I just want to go home. *We all* just want to go home." Carter held on to Arthur. Creepy Leaf Girl pointed at the shears now, and then at the fountain of water behind Mr. Green. She was trying to get Carter to do something.

Mr. Green wasn't watching her. He had his eyes very keenly on Carter. His horrible, unblinking wooden eyes.

"Hmmm. Yes, no doubt you do want to go home. But there's a price. No one leaves the curious maze without paying. It's quite a simple price, though. All you have to do is answer these questions truthfully, and I'll let you go: Are you *scared* now? Was this afternoon *boring*? Or was the curious maze the most *interesting* ride at the fair?"

Carter frowned. *Scared*? No kidding! *Boring*? Hardly! *Interesting*? Yes!

But there was a stubborn place in Carter that suddenly dug in its heels. He and Arthur had been through so much. Why did Mr. Green get to say when they go home? What gave him the right to scare them? So Carter said, "You have no right to do this to us. Now send us home!" He hoped he sounded brave, but in the deep forest with creepy Mr. Green standing there ... he probably didn't.

Mr. Green stood in a stray shaft of sunlight that filtered down through the trees. It was almost sundown, and soon the forest would be pitch black. The fountain burbled at Mr. Green's feet. Behind him, Creepy Leaf Girl gestured wildly at the garden shears.

The old man drew in close to Carter, and there was no doubt about it now: his eyes WERE made of wood. He blinked, and they clicked like marbles. Carter drew back in horror.

The old man laughed, or rather, creaked and moaned.

"You will wander the curious maze forever, like Clarissa here, until you answer me!"

Clarissa?

The old man closed his eyes and threw
his head back to take another drink from the
fountain. Leaves sprouted from his hair, his
eyebrows, his ears, his hands ....

Now, Carter!

Carter lunged forward and grabbed the
garden shears.

He tossed them through the air and they
flipped end over end over end. With a fantastic
leap, Clarissa caught them.

Then she plunged the garden shears deep
into the fountain.

SPLOOSH! The water bubbled, burned
and rose, higher and higher.

"No! NO!" the old man screamed. He threw
his arms deep into the pool, frantically grasping
for the shears hidden in the dark water. Clarissa
ran up, pushed with all her might ... and Mr.
Green toppled and fell into the fountain.

One. Two. Three. Four seconds, and still
no Mr. Green. The water bubbled, fumed,
and roiled, rising angrily. Five seconds, six
... seven, eight ... the water rose higher and
Carter held his breath.

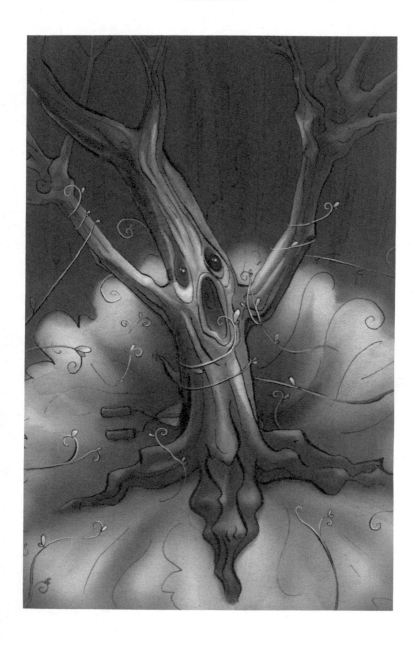

…nine, ten, eleven, twelve …

… then a figure burst out of the pool. A twig man stepped stiffly out of the water, leafy arms held out.

The boys backed up in horror. The twig man took a few more stiff steps toward them, and then suddenly his leafy right arm jerked toward the sky. Then his left arm followed. The look of surprise froze on the twig man's face as it turned to tree bark. His feet grew into long roots that dove into the earth. With a huge *CRACK,* his arms grew and grew, and his chest thickened and lengthened as the tree trunk stretched toward the stars. His knees turned into tree limbs, his shoulders into huge boughs, his hair into leafy branches and twigs.

The figure crashed upward through the other trees, snapping, creaking, and breaking through everything in its path.

Right before their eyes, Mr. Green turned into an enormous and ancient tree.

Before he disappeared completely, the old man's voice carried on the wind: *and here is the end of the curious maze!*

CHAPTER 16

HERE IS THE END

The forest fell silent, the fountain was gone, and the huge tree that was once Mr. Green stood shoulder-to-shoulder with the other trees.

Carter, Clarissa, and Arthur looked at each other.

What just happened?

Clarissa spoke first. "Thank you, Carter. You saved us. I've been waiting for someone to toss me the old man's garden shears for ages!"

"What do you mean, 'waiting for some-one?' Who? Who have you been waiting for?"

"You don't think you're the only person to get caught in the curious maze, do you? Mr.

Green has chosen many bored children for the maze over the years. But most of them just tell Mr. Green what he wants to hear. That they were *scared*. That the maze is *interesting*. That there's nothing *dull* about it. And then they return to their own time like nothing happened."

"Well, why are *you* still here?"

Clarissa shrugged. "I don't get scared that easily, I guess. I just couldn't lie and tell him I was scared. So I've been stuck in this maze for a long time. But as you just saw, there is more than one way out of a maze."

"There are two ways?"

Clarissa pointed at the old man's red-handled garden shears, lying on the forest floor where the fountain was a moment before. "The garden shears were the key to the magic of the maze. One way out of the maze was to tell Mr. Green you're scared. The other way out was to hide his magic garden shears, even for a moment. But I could never get close to them, the old man guarded them so well. You must have noticed that. I knew the maze would end if I could hide them in the fountain even for a second, but I didn't know he'd turn into a tree if he got pushed in. That was a stroke of luck."

The children all looked at the tree that was once Mr. Green and quickly looked away.

"Well … why haven't I seen the maze before? I come to the fair every year."

Clarissa put her head on one side and smiled a little. "You ask a lot of questions. The maze is an ancient and magical creation. It never stays in one place for long. Or one time."

Carter was going to ask what she meant, but something was happening to Clarissa. She was shimmering and slowly, slowly, she faded away. For a second, he saw her standing in front of the curious maze on a sunny summer day … and a man and woman called her name. Her parents? She ran over to them, and then the image vanished. The last thing Carter saw was the smile on her face.

Then the little hand he held let go. Arthur was fading, too! Slowly the little boy shimmered and faded, just like Clarissa. As he vanished, he locked eyes with Carter and raised his pudgy hand in goodbye.

Then Carter heard a woman's voice say, "There you are, Arthur! You've lost your cap!"

And a little voice answered, "Mummy!"

"See you, Arthur!" Carter whispered to the dark, empty forest.

At that moment the sun vanished, and Carter was left completely alone. The forest fell into blackness.

His heart started to pound, and his mouth went dry. He walked over to the garden shears and picked them up. They were warm and heavy, and he could almost feel the old man's hand upon them, which instantly made him want to put them down. He leaned them against the bottom of the tree that was Mr. Green.

"Mr. Green! If you can hear me ... now it's my turn! I want to go home, too!" he called.

The forest grew darker ... and small rustlings began to fill the air. He tried to stay calm.

THINK, CARTER!

What was he supposed to do? He thought about entering the maze (how long ago that seemed!), about meeting Arthur, Clarissa, and the wounded soldier, how the Native boy saved him, about his sister calling him again and again. He thought about all of it. He'd seen what scary was, he knew now that the haunted house *was* for kids. But there was nothing wrong with that, since little kids need haunted houses to get them ready for bigger, scarier things. There were still plenty of strange surprises out there to amaze and delight a person. More than he could possibly imagine.

"Mr. Green?" he called quietly.

A single leaf fluttered down from the tree that was once Mr. Green. It landed gently at Carter's feet. He stooped and picked it up.

"Mr. Green? If you're listening, the curious maze was definitely the most interesting thing that's ever happened to me." It suddenly struck him that despite the terror, the fear, the strangeness of it all, it *had* been the most exciting day of his life.

Another leaf fluttered down and landed at his feet. He cleared his throat and raised his voice a little.

"But Clarissa, Arthur, and I got to the end of the maze, you said so yourself. You also said we could leave when we got to the end, unless you intend to cheat. They've both gone back to their own time. And now I'd just really like to go home, too." A few more leaves fluttered down at his feet.

"I don't think what you did was right, but the truth is ... I *was* scared. I still am. But I was more than just that. I've had to be brave, and smart, and curious, too. And I couldn't give up, even though I really wanted to. The maze *was* the best ride at the fair, the best ride I could imagine. Ever."

It was true, all of it.

Then with a tiny click, a door opened at the bottom of the tree that was Mr. Green. A warm light shone from behind the door, the kind of light that made Carter think of sunshine and a summer day.

He walked across the dark forest, stepped through the door ...

... and stood at the opening of a very familiar, leafy pathway.

Carter was back at the beginning of his strange afternoon. Just like that, he had found his way out of the curious maze.

CHAPTER 17

THAT WHICH IS MOST CURIOUS

Carter stood at the entrance to the curious maze in the exact spot where he stood earlier that day, before the whole crazy afternoon began. The sun was a little lower in the sky, maybe, but apart from that, nothing had changed from the moment he entered the maze.

Moments before? Hours before? A lifetime ago?

Huge roller coasters whizzed over his head, their giant wheels squealing. People shrieked as they whipped by, children ate ice cream (in cones!), cars drove past, airplanes zoomed overhead. Carter wanted to hug everyone he saw, wanted to spin in circles laughing, but he didn't.

I'm back!

"CARTER! CARTER!" a voice called. It was Sydney! She waved. "Over here!"

He ran to his sister. Then for the first time since he was seven years old, he gave her a huge hug. He could honestly say that he'd never been so happy to see her, or her amazingly weird red squid hat.

"What? What the heck's wrong with you? Are you okay?" she asked, surprised. Carter was glad that she hugged him back, though, just a little.

"I ... I'm not sure," he said. "Probably not, no, not really." Sydney ignored him and pointed at the "Welcome to the Curious Maze" signpost.

"I think that's false advertising: the most interesting ride you'll ever take? Hardly."

Carter didn't know whether he should laugh or scream. Was she kidding? He looked at his sister, still feeling strange and dizzy, but she didn't seem to be joking with him.

"Sydney, I've been gone for hours in that maze. Haven't you missed me?"

"What do you mean? 'Gone for hours?'

And why would I miss you? I've been right here, calling you. You were only gone a few minutes. What's wrong with you? You don't look too well." She looked at him, a little concerned. Carter shook his head. He couldn't quite grasp what was happening.

"Um, did you go into the maze, too?" he asked, a little breathless.

Sydney looked at him very closely. "I went in, walked to the exit, then came out. You took a little longer but came out a few minutes later. Are you okay, little brother? Do you have sunstroke or something?"

Carter felt faint. What was going on?

"Did you see Mr. Green, too?"

"Mr. Green? Who's that? I don't know what you're talking about, Carter." She spoke very slowly and clearly like she would to a small child who didn't quite understand what was being said. "You and I went for a walk over to the maze for a few minutes, and then I got through the maze first, and you followed a few minutes later. I called you a few times, then there you were. Why would I worry about you in a maze for ten minutes?"

"You … you've been standing here the whole time? You didn't miss me?" he asked.

"Yes, Carter, I've been standing here the whole time. And no I didn't miss you. There was no time to miss you. Geesh, now I know you have sunstroke." Sydney had clearly had enough of the conversation and took one last look at the curious maze sign. "Hardly the most interesting ride ever," she muttered. "It's almost four o'clock. Let's go find Mom. Maybe take you to the hospital and get your brain checked," she teased. Then she walked away.

Carter gulped. Okay. So it was all a hallucination? A bizarre, terrifying dream? A trick of the light?

No! Arthur, Clarissa, the freak show, the grand magazine explosion, the bear, the old French fort. Mr. Green. It was REAL. He was THERE. Time passed differently in the maze. Maybe what took an afternoon for him just took a few minutes for Sydney, but it still happened.

Carter's head was spinning. He was glad to be back … but nothing made sense.

He ran to catch up with his sister, and they headed toward the parking lot to find their mother.

The late afternoon sun shone on the midway, lighting up the huge roller coasters and

Ferris wheels in the distance. People sat on picnic benches eating an early dinner, or ice cream. In cones.

Maybe it was all a dream?

Carter took a deep breath and tried to calm down. It was okay. Whatever had happened to him that afternoon, he was back, he was safe. It had been a strange adventure, but he found his way out of the maze. It was over.

He didn't look back. Then he did, just once … and did a double-take.

Carter gasped. Then he tried not to scream.

A tiny figure in a green smock stood beside a tree and waved at him.

The figure clutched a pair of red-handled garden shears!

Carter didn't *want* to see, didn't *want* to hear, didn't *want* to know. But he knew all the same. There was no denying what he just saw. Or what he knew was coming next.

Just below the screams of the midway, there it was, the sound he'd never forget for as long as he lived …

SNIP!

SNIP!

Then, as Carter watched in horror, Mr. Green and the curious maze disappeared in a whirlwind of dust, off to startle and astound children in another fairground, in some other far-away place and long-ago time.

THIS PART IS (ALSO) MOSTLY TRUE

Welcome to the end of the story, and if you've made it this far, congratulations. I told you at the beginning that it was scary and more than a little strange, yet here you are. I'm sure you'll never look at a leafy garden maze the same way ever again.

You've no doubt got many questions at this point. You're probably wondering what happened next, and you might also be thinking … is this story true?

Well, some parts of it are absolutely true. Still, if you remember on the very first pages of this book, you read these words: Truth is an odd thing. One person's truth can be another person's lie. That's the most important thing to remember about this story: sometimes things that seem like lies are actually true. And sometimes, you never can tell.

Truth can be sneaky, although that shouldn't stop anyone from seeking it. So without further ado, here are some definite truths …

… freak shows were a regular feature of fairs in the past, battles from long ago did occur in many strange and unlikely places, and Native families traded with Europeans a long time before there were cities.

But I suspect what you really want to know is far less factual, and much more strange. No doubt you want to know if there really was an Arthur, a Creepy Leaf Girl, a wounded soldier, and a young Native boy wandering around a curious, leafy maze?

Was Carter really there in all those time periods, hearing and seeing all the things that had happened in that same spot over hundreds of years?

Well, time travel is a tricky business. Who knows the journeys others take in their spare time on a sunny summer afternoon? I can tell you this, though: I, for one, would give a good deal to visit a fair in my city over one hundred years ago, or to spend an afternoon among the traders and Native families of a very old and little-known French trading post. The battle-ground I could skip, quite frankly, since I have little stomach for such things.

You only need to read a good book on the subject at hand to decide what's real and what's not, or dare I say, even feel as though you'd been transported there yourself for a while.

And finally ... what about Mr. Green? Did he use the magic garden shears that Carter so kindly propped against him to turn back into himself? Let's just say that the maze is a kind of game, after all, and a very ancient one at that. It could have magic at its roots somewhere, and someone has to trim it and care for it. If the maze-keeper chose children who were bored with the usual ideas of fun to teach them what interesting really means, that just adds to the curious nature of his story, doesn't it?

I CAN tell you that every once in a while, a peculiar story will pop up about a strange maze-keeper and a vanishing maze. And every once in very long while, the story may include a rattled child spouting an odd tale about time travel, a small man in a green smock and magical garden shears. As for the truth? The only way to know for sure is to look for an inviting leafy green pathway the next time you're at the fair ... and consider taking a journey of your own.

Now you know the story of Carter and the curious maze. Despite his experience that day, Carter grew up to have a pretty normal life. He was an expert historian, by the way, and taught history classes at the local university, specializing in early European and Native trade.

There were only two things a little strange about Carter.

One: he never (EVER) went anywhere near a fairground or midway ever again. The sight of an old-fashioned carousel could send him into a frenzy.

Two: Garden shears were strictly forbidden. Even large scissors would upset him. But worse than that, sometimes in the middle of the night he would sit bolt upright in bed and call out to his family: "Do you hear someone TRIMMING THE HEDGE?"

A HISTORICAL NOTE FROM THE AUTHOR

The fairground in this book is full of mysterious secrets. In fact, all the events described in this story are based on real historical events that occurred on the fairground near the lake by my home, and all the time periods that Carter visits in this book have been carefully researched.

The Grand Fair in 1903 is an accurate depiction of many North American agricultural fairs at the time. The sideshow freaks, rides, and food are all historically correct. There really was a Wild Man of Borneo, and Thumbelina really was billed as the smallest mother in the world in 1903, for example.

The soldier's fort is a real place, and there was a battle between American and British soldiers there on April 27, 1813. The battle ended when the British blew up the Grand Magazine, which resulted in the largest man-made explosion the world had ever experienced up until that time, and wounded or killed almost five hundred American, British, and Native soldiers in a few moments.

Finally, a tiny trading fort stood on the same fairgrounds over two hundred and fifty years ago, where the French traded with Native hunters. A small memorial marker stands on the fairgrounds today, recognizing the existence of the Fort from 1750–59.

With a little digging, you'll likely discover that your local fairground is just as interesting and strange as mine. I hope you enjoy many curious and wonderful summer adventures there!

— Philippa Dowding

The author would like to thank the staff at Fort York and CNE Archives for their helpful insight.

They're troubling. They're bizarre.
And they JUST might be true …

Weird Stories Gone Wrong

BY PHILIPPA DOWDING

BOOK 1
The ghastly truth about
a giant hand …

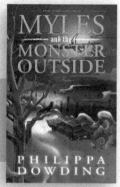

BOOK 2
A rainy night,
a haunted highway,
a mysterious monster …

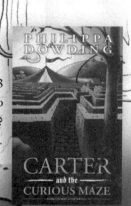

BOOK 3
Are you brave enough to
enter the curious maze?
Not everyone comes out …

*Three tremendously terrifying tales you'll want to share with your
enemies (should you want to scare them silly) …*

ALSO BY AWARD-WINNING AUTHOR PHILIPPA DOWDING

. . . .

THE LOST GARGOYLE SERIES

THE GARGOYLE IN MY YARD

What do you do when a 400-year-old gargoyle moves into your backyard? Especially when no one else but you knows he's ALIVE? Twelve-year-old Katherine Newberry can tell you all about life with a gargoyle. He's naughty and gets others into trouble. But if you're like Katherine, after getting to know him, you might really want him to stay.

Commended for the 2009 Resource Links Best Books, for the 2010 Best Books for Kids and Teens, and shortlisted for the 2011 Diamond Willow Award.

THE GARGOYLE OVERHEAD

What if your best friend was a naughty 400-year-old gargoyle? And what if he just happened to be in terrible danger? Its not always easy, but thirteen-year-old Katherine Newberry is friends with a gargoyle who has lost his greatest friend. Gargoth's greatest enemy is prowling the city, and it's a race against time to find her first!

Shortlisted for the 2012 Silver Birch Express Award.

THE GARGOYLE AT THE GATES

Christopher is astonished to discover that gargoyles Ambergine and Gargoth are living in the park next door and that Katherine, a girl from his class, knows the gargoyles, as well. When the Collector steals Ambergine, it's up to Christopher and Katherine to get her back, as long as something else doesn't catch them along the way.

Shortlisted for the Hackmatack Children's Choice Book Award, the 2013 Diamond Willow Award, and commended for the 2013 White Raven Award.